Every new generation of children is enthralled by the famous stories in our Well-Loved Tales series. Younger ones love to have the story read to them, and to examine each tiny detail of the full colour illustrations. Older children will enjoy the exciting stories in an easy-to-read text.

Pinocchio
by Carlo Collodi

retold for easy reading
by AUDREY DALY

illustrated by MARTIN AITCHISON

Ladybird Books Loughborough

This is the strange story of a piece of wood — that became a puppet — that became a real live boy!

It all started when Antonio the carpenter took a piece of wood from the pile in the corner of his workshop. It was quite an ordinary piece of wood — nothing much to look at. Then as Antonio raised his sharp axe to take off the bark, a little voice said, "Please don't hit me too hard!"

Antonio was afraid. He looked all round his workshop, then down at the piece of wood. "No, no," he thought. "I'm dreaming." And lifting his axe once more, he hit the piece of wood very hard.

"Oh, you've *hurt* me!" cried the same little voice.

Now Antonio was really frightened, but just at that moment his friend Geppetto came to the door. Geppetto had no children of his own, and he wanted a piece of wood to make into a puppet that could dance and jump and move just like a real boy.

Thankfully Antonio gave him the piece of wood that had given him such a fright. Geppetto went off with it happily and began to make his new puppet right away. " I shall call him Pinocchio," he thought as he worked. " That's a good name."

As soon as he made the puppet's face, its eyes moved, and its mouth laughed. Then as Geppetto finished the feet, Pinocchio kicked him on the nose.

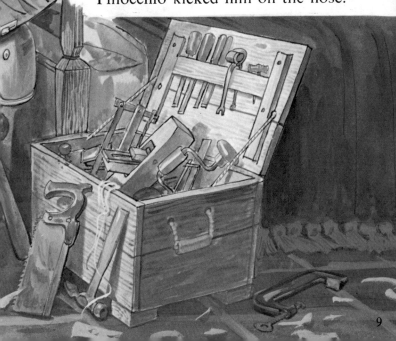

Geppetto was pleased with his new puppet, in spite of its tricks. He showed Pinocchio how to walk, one foot in front of the other. Instantly the puppet ran into the street! Geppetto ran after him, but he was too slow.

Pinocchio ran along the street and straight into the arms of a policeman! The policeman gave him back to Geppetto, but the other people in the street felt sorry for Pinocchio. They said that Geppetto was a bully. The policeman listened to them, and he took Geppetto to prison.

While poor Geppetto was being taken to prison for something he hadn't done, Pinocchio ran home. He lay down in the house, very pleased with himself.

Then he heard a little voice not far away. Pinocchio was frightened. He turned and saw a big cricket walking slowly up the wall.

"I'm the Talking Cricket," it said. "There's something I must tell you. Boys who turn against their fathers and run away from home are always sorry for it in the end."

"Chirp away, Cricket," said Pinocchio. "It makes no difference to me what you say. I'm running away from here tomorrow. If I don't I shall have to go to school like other boys. I don't want to learn anything. I don't want to work. All I want to do is have a good time."

The Cricket sighed. "I'm really sorry for you, Pinocchio. You'll end up in prison."

This made Pinocchio so cross that he threw a hammer at the Cricket — and the Cricket vanished.

Now Pinocchio was hungry, for he had eaten nothing all day. The only food in the house was an egg, but when Pinocchio tried to cook it, a chicken hatched out and flew away.

He set out into the wet stormy night to find food, but no one would give him any. At last he went home, put his feet by the fire to dry them, and fell sound asleep.

Of course Pinocchio's feet were made of wood, so bit by bit they burnt away as he slept.

Suddenly there was a knock at the door. It was Geppetto!

The puppet tried to run to open the door — and fell on the floor. "I can't open it," he shouted. "My feet have gone."

Geppetto was very cross as he climbed through the window. He thought Pinocchio was playing another of his tricks. Then he saw that the puppet really had no feet, and he was sorry.

19

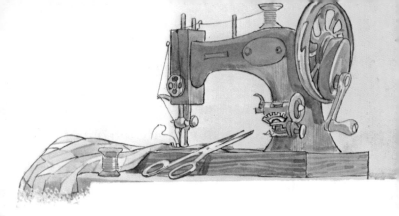

Pinocchio was so hungry that Geppetto gave him his own breakfast of three pears. As soon as he had eaten them however, the puppet began to ask for new feet.

Geppetto wanted to teach him a lesson though, so he left him to cry for a long time.

At last Pinocchio promised to be good and go to school, and Geppetto made him two beautiful new feet. He even made him some clothes for school.

All Pinocchio needed now was a spelling book, but there was no money to buy one.

Geppetto was sad because he couldn't help. Then he had an idea. He ran out of the house into the snow, putting on his old coat as he went.

Soon he came back — with a spelling book, but without his coat. He had sold his coat to buy the book for his puppet son!

As soon as the snow stopped, Pinocchio set out for school. As he went, he told himself that one day he would earn lots of money to buy Geppetto a really beautiful coat to repay him.

Suddenly there was the sound of music in the distance. What could it be? Pinocchio stood still, listening. Then he made up his mind. He could always go to school tomorrow instead.

He ran towards the sound of the music.

The music came from the Great Puppet Theatre! But Pinocchio had no money to go in. He thought for a moment, then he sold his spelling book for twopence. Poor Geppetto, shivering at home in the cold because he bought Pinocchio a spelling book!

Pinocchio had forgotten all about Geppetto however. As he went into the theatre he felt really at home. The puppets welcomed him as a long lost brother and the play stopped as they said hello.

The puppets had a master called Fire-eater. He was very fierce, with a long black beard. He saw that the play had stopped because of Pinocchio, and he was angry.

At first he was going to throw Pinocchio on the fire. Then he decided to forgive him, and to put Harlequin on the fire.

But brave Pinocchio said he would die instead, and at last the Fire-eater forgave them both.

The puppets were so happy at this that they clapped and clapped. Then they danced merrily all night.

Next day Fire-eater gave Pinocchio five
gold coins to take to his father Geppetto,
and sent him home very pleased with himself.

Pinocchio was determined to be good this time, but he was soon in trouble again. He met a wicked Fox who pretended to be lame, and a Cat who pretended to be blind. They tried to steal his money, but he ran away from them.

The villains chased Pinocchio
and tried to stab him. Luckily the puppet
was made of such hard wood that their
knives broke!

They were so cross that they hanged him
from an oak tree and left him to die.

As Pinocchio swung from the tree, a little
girl with blue hair saw him from her house
nearby. She was really a Fairy in disguise,
and she sent her servants to help the puppet.

The Fairy gave Pinocchio some medicine to make him well, then she asked him his story. Pinocchio told the truth to start with. Then when he came to the gold pieces, he told a lie. He said he had lost them, but they were in his pocket!

As soon as he told this lie, Pinocchio's nose grew two inches longer! Then he told another lie — and his nose grew longer still, and went on growing.

The puppet's nose grew so long because of his lies that he couldn't get out of the door.

The Fairy laughed and laughed at Pinocchio as she watched, and he began to cry. He cried and cried for a long time before the Fairy forgave him for telling lies. Then at last she called in some woodpeckers to help him. They pecked and pecked at his nose until it was the right length again, and Pinocchio was happy once more.

The Fairy was fond of Pinocchio, even
though he was so naughty. She wanted him
to stay with her. Pinocchio said he was going
home to his father Geppetto, but the Fairy
said that Geppetto was coming to stay too!

Pinocchio was so pleased and excited when he heard this that he set out to meet Geppetto. He hadn't seen him for such a long time.

Pinocchio was looking forward to seeing Geppetto again, but it was not to be. The wicked Fox and Cat turned up once more, and stole his gold pieces. When Pinocchio told a policeman about it, *he* was put in prison — for four whole months. He couldn't understand this at all.

When he came out of prison, the puppet went back to find the Fairy. When he came to the right place, the house was nowhere to be seen!

As Pinocchio stood there crying because his Fairy had gone, a Pigeon flew down. It told him that Geppetto was so unhappy that he had gone to sea in a boat to look for Pinocchio. This made the puppet cry even more because he missed Geppetto too.

The Pigeon was sorry for him. It took him on its back to the sea to find Geppetto. Once more Pinocchio was unlucky — a Dolphin told him that Geppetto had been swallowed by a terrible Shark!

Now Pinocchio found himself on an island where everyone worked so hard that they were called Busy Bees. Pinocchio was hungry — but *he* wasn't going to work for his food.

Soon he was so hungry that he *had* to work. He helped a woman to carry some water. When she gave him some food, he saw she was his own Fairy! He had found her again.

Pinocchio told the Fairy he was tired of being a puppet. He wanted to become a real live boy.

She said he could only become a real boy if he was good and obedient. He must never tell lies, and he must go to school. So Pinocchio went to school. He worked so

hard that he became top of his class, and the Fairy was pleased. She promised that soon he would become a real boy.

But there were bad boys in the class. They led him astray and — Pinocchio ran away again!

This time he went to Toyland with some other naughty boys. They were all changed into Donkeys — ears, tails and all!

Pinocchio became a donkey in a circus. One day he fell and hurt his leg as he was jumping through the hoop. This made him lame, so he was sold for his skin to be made into a drum.

His new master threw him into the sea to drown — and he became a puppet again.

Pinocchio's adventures still weren't over.
As he lay at the bottom of the sea, he was
swallowed by a Shark. It was the same
terrible Shark that had swallowed his father
Geppetto — and Geppetto was still alive!
Pinocchio made a plan, and led him out
through the Shark's mouth to safety.

Now Pinocchio worked so hard to look after his poor father that the Fairy forgave him for the third and last time, and gave him his wish.

So — at last — he became a real live boy.